MASTER of MAHOGANY

MASTER of MAHOGANY

TOM DAY, FREE BLACK CABINETMAKER

MARY E. LYONS

CHARLES SCRIBNER'S SONS • NEW YORK
Maxwell Macmillan Canada • Toronto
Maxwell Macmillan International
New York • Oxford • Singapore • Sydney

ACKNOWLEDGMENTS

I am indebted to the National Endowment for the Humanities and the DeWitt Wallace Reader's Digest Fund. Their Teacher-Scholar Award provided the time and financial support necessary to begin research on the life of Tom Day. I am also grateful to the curatorial staff of Colonial Williamsburg and to Michael Nicholls of the University of Utah for sharing their expertise.

Special thanks to these helpful citizens of Caswell County, North Carolina: Elizabeth and Tom McPherson, owners of the Woodside Inn Bed and Breakfast, Margaret and Ben Williams, Hattie May Thompson, George Scott, Marian Thomas, Mary Satterfield, Jean Scott, and other members of the Thomas Day House / Union Tavern Restoration Committee, P.O. Box 1996, Milton, North Carolina 27305.

Text copyright © 1994 by Mary E. Lyons

Charles Scribner's Sons Books for Young Readers
Macmillan Publishing Company
866 Third Avenue, New York, NY 10022

Maxwell Macmillan Canada, Inc.
1200 Eglinton Avenue East, Suite 200
Don Mills, Ontario M3C 3N1

Macmillan Publishing Company is part of the Maxwell Communication Group of Companies.
First edition   10 9 8 7 6 5 4 3 2 1
Printed in Hong Kong on recycled paper.
Book design by Vikki Sheatsley

Library of Congress Cataloging-in-Publication Data
Lyons, Mary (Mary E.)
   Master of mahogany : Tom Day, free Black cabinet-
maker / Mary E. Lyons .   —1st ed.   p.   cm.
   Includes bibliographical references and index.
   ISBN 0-684-19675-1
1. Day, Tom, 1801–ca. 1861—Juvenile literature. 2. Afro-American cabinetmakers—Biography—Juvenile literature. [1. Day, Tom, 1801–ca. 1861. 2. Furniture workers. 3. Afro-Americans—Biography.]   I. Title.
NK2439.D38L96 1994   749.213—dc20   [B]   93-37900
SUMMARY: A biography of Tom Day, nineteenth-century African-American cabinetmaker

To Arthur Collier

The boys in this 1853 painting are using a two-man cross-cut saw. Two adults may have started the cut, then turned the job over to the children. *Abby Aldrich Rockefeller Folk Art Center, Williamsburg, Virginia.*

FOREWORD

The woods seemed alive to Tom Day when he was a boy in Virginia in the early 1800s. Whiskery old pines whistled hello in the spring and spit pinecones in the fall. Before a winter storm, young beeches trembled like coatless children. And when the woodsman's ax brought an oak to its knees, a crack of surprised pain echoed through the forest.

Tom winced every time a proud tree crashed to the ground. But he knew that the fallen giants would come to life again. This was the age of wood, when a friend or neighbor was likely to be a carpenter, carver, or cooper. With a few hand tools and a lot of skill, these craftsmen turned huge logs into barrels, brooms, cabinets, coaches, shakes, and shingles.

The older men would have let a boy like Tom watch, help, and learn. He piled planks crosswise in flat stacks for air-drying. He fetched, cleaned, and oiled tools. At the sawmill he balanced on top of a log that stretched across the saw pit. A pitman stood underneath. Each time the man raked the saw down—*scrit!*, Tom pulled it up again—*scrat!*

Perhaps Tom was sweeping sawdust out of a cabinetmaker's workshop when he saw the future in his mind. One day he would be his own boss—not a pupil, but a teacher. Not a beginner, but an expert. He, too, would become a master of wood.

Two Greek columns support this mantel by Tom Day. He streaked the wooden columns with brown, white, and red paint to make them look like marble. *Jim Bridges*.

Each column is topped with a Greek Ionic capital. *Jim Bridges.*

The Indentured Years
· 1801–1822 ·

Tom Day's history is like a piece of furniture before it is finished. A few of the parts are complete and glide smoothly into place. Others are the result of guesswork, with only a rough fit. Some sections are missing altogether. Because the history of many nineteenth-century African Americans was not written down, Tom's entire story may never be known. But we can assemble enough fragments to recreate the whole.

We know that his birthplace was Halifax County, Virginia. He was born in 1801 when his mother, Morning S. Day, was thirty-five years old. Local legend says that one of her parents was Native American and that her full name was Morning Star Day.

Tom was an educated person who could read and write. Somehow he learned to make furniture, mantels, doorways, and other final woodwork for a house. Most important for an African American living in a slave state, Thomas Day was born free because his mother was free.

Morning Star may have been from one of the free black families who had lived in southern, or Southside, Virginia since the 1600s. It is possible, but not likely, that she was born enslaved, then released after she turned eighteen. A 1782 Virginia law permitted slaveholders to free healthy slaves between the ages of eighteen and forty-five. Few slaves in Southside, however, were let go as a result of the law. Morning Star might also have been left free in her slaveholder's will.

Free blacks, especially women, were barely free at all. Many lived like slaves. The county courts in Southside usually required that they be indentured, or bound out, as servants to a white person. So a free woman like Morning Star might have lived in the house of a white master who also owned slaves.

If Morning Star was indentured, Tom would have been indentured, too. It was customary for a master to provide his indentured servants with food, clothing, shelter, and a year of schooling. This would explain how Tom learned to read and write. A different master may have introduced Tom to woodworking; the courts often apprenticed free black children to a white man who could teach them a trade.

It is also possible that Tom's father taught him. The identity of his father is a mystery, and there are few clues to help solve the puzzle. The name "Tom Day" was a common one in eighteenth-century Virginia. It appears in several advertisements for runaway slaves. We can imagine that one of them was the father of Tom Day the cabinetmaker.

In the spring of 1780 an advertisement in a Maryland newspaper offered a reward for a runaway slave carpenter named Tom Day. This particular Tom Day had escaped from Virginia with eleven other artisan slaves.

The group of four women and eight men were skilled in everything from shoemaking to gardening to weaving and spinning. They included a man named Cyrus, who wore "a very remarkable coat, having a great number of patches of different colours . . . They are most of them very artful," said the advertisement, "and expect to pass as free people." The runaways headed north toward Baltimore.

Slave escapes were often unsuccessful. This group was resourceful, but perhaps too large to pass unnoticed—especially if Cyrus could not part with his coat of many colors. Day may have been caught and sent back into slavery by his slaveholder, Burgess Ball. But then how would the carpenter have found his way to Halifax County and Morning Star?

Ball owned property less than seventy miles from Halifax County, Virginia. After his death in 1800, Ball's widow settled his estate, and perhaps sold the valuable slave carpenter to someone in nearby Halifax, where he could have met Morning Star. Their son, Thomas Day, was born a year later in 1801.

Whoever taught Tom carpentry would have noticed his fascination with wood and his good eye for design. Like other boys of his day, he liked to shoot marbles, play ball, and fly kites. But carving with a pocketknife was just as much fun. A fellow could spend hours whittling curlicues out of chunks of soft pine. Tom probably used a pocketknife to practice making his favorite shape—a deeply curved scroll that looks like a giant's thumb.

If young Tom was apprenticed, he settled in for about four years of struggle and sweat. This was the usual length of time for an apprenticeship in America. He would have slept in the master's shop, where the sharp-edged smell of raw wood tickled his nose at night, and sawdust sifted like snow into his hair. If the master had any slaves, Tom took his meals in the kitchen with them.

Even with his instinct for woodworking, the first thing he would have learned was how much there was to learn! Tom didn't know a **bench dog*** from a hound dog. And what was a **donkey's ear**? He discovered the difference between a rabbit and a **rabbet** and how to tell a **slat** from a **splat**.

Tom already knew how to read books. Now he learned to read wood. At the sawmill he rejected planks of wood with loose knots that could fall out as the board dried. He avoided split wood damaged by frost. He also learned the best wood for each job. White pine, which grew everywhere, was fine for ordinary furniture. Maple was prized for its creamy beauty, and imported mahogany was favored for carving.

He learned how to make animal glue: Take the waste pieces of skin, horn, and hooves

*See glossary at the back of the book for definitions of *bench dog* and other terms printed in bold type.

The top of this mahogany chair shows Tom's favorite thumblike decoration. Early American furniture makers and architects often used a similar design, which was of English origin. *North Carolina State Archives, Raleigh, North Carolina.*

from an ox. Steep, wash, and boil. Then strain, melt, reboil, and mold the mixture into square cakes. The older the ox, the stronger the glue.

Most important, Tom learned the three basic methods of joining wood together to make a piece of furniture: panel construction for doors, **mortise and tenon** joints for chairs, and interlocking **dovetails** for drawers.

With the help of glue, these timeless methods have been used to build furniture for thousands of years. Although machines do the work now, the same joints can still be found in better makes of modern furniture. If you pull a drawer out of a chest, you may find dovetail joints where the front and sides meet.

According to Virginia law, Tom's indenture had to end when he was twenty-one years old. On reaching this age, every free black in Virginia was required to register at the county courthouse. In 1822 Tom would have done the same.

For twenty-five cents, the clerk of the Halifax County court issued a set of handwritten free papers to Tom, then stamped them with an official seal. Tom Day had to carry these papers in his pocket for the rest of his life. They were his only legal protection against slavery.

By the age of twenty-one, he would have known the basics of cabinetry, but not the artistry. Several cabinetmakers lived just over the state line in the village of Milton, North Carolina. Maybe one of them would teach him how to carve a snake foot, a turnip foot, an onion foot, and a claw foot. In exchange, Tom would work for the cabinetmaker as a journeyman, or paid craftsman.

Tom's decision to leave was an expensive one. A 1795 North Carolina law required that he post a bond of two hundred pounds for "good behavior" in order to enter the state. But it was no longer safe to stay in Virginia.

In 1823 that state passed a new rule. A free black found guilty of almost any crime could be sold into slavery as punishment. Tom

Tom glued together panels of cheap wood to make the double door at Woodside. Then he painted the door with a false grain to give it the appearance of expensive wood. *Jim Bridges.*

An apprentice often made a miniature piece like this one constructed by Tom Day. The chest proved that he was a master of cabinetmaking skills. *William Edmund Barrett.*

thought that spending the money was a bargain compared to the risk of losing his freedom. Besides, many free blacks slipped over the line without paying the bond. Maybe he could, too.

It must have been hard to think about leaving the young beauty Acquilla Wilson. Five years younger than Tom, Acquilla was a member of the free black community in Halifax County. He had probably known her all his life. Now she was seventeen and old enough to marry.

Perhaps Tom thought there was time enough for marriage after he had learned all the tricks of his trade. Would Acquilla wait for him? They would be separated by only a few miles, but many years might keep them from becoming husband and wife.

Local tradition says that Tom moved to Milton in 1823. He came to stay for four years. By 1827, he figured, he would know enough to make furniture by himself. He would also have enough money saved to start a business somewhere else in North Carolina. And finally he and Acquilla could be married.

If the tall, handsome, young man could have peeked into the future, he would have

The heavily carved feet of this writing table look like an animal's paws. *North Carolina State Archives, Raleigh, North Carolina.*

been surprised. Almost thirty years later he wrote to his daughter, "I came here to stay four years and am here 7 time 4. . . ." Thomas Day became Milton's most famous resident, and he lived there for the rest of his life.

The Journeyman Years
• 1823–1827 •

When Tom crossed Country Line Creek into North Carolina, he found a state that seemed to be asleep. Some visitors even called it the Rip van Winkle State. While other states had been building schools and passable roads, "Old Rip" had been napping.

Most counties had no public schools, and the deeply rutted roads were little more than cow paths. Few free blacks in Halifax County owned horses. When Tom set out from Halifax County, for Milton, he probably walked. If it rained along the way, he slogged through mud to get there.

North Carolinians often used rivers instead of roads to move people and goods. The stately Dan River flowed like a highway from Virginia into Caswell County, North Carolina, just a mile from Tom's new home of Milton. The bottomland along the river was the richest soil in the county. And the farmers along the river were the richest men.

Slaves loaded the farmers' tobacco crops onto flat-bottomed boats called *bateaux*.

Then black crews floated and pushed the tobacco to larger towns downstream to sell it at auction. When Tom arrived in Milton, the small village had become a center of this tobacco economy.

As he strolled along Main Street and down side alleys, he passed a caravan of other shops: Jesse Owen's Saddlery, the Milton Book Store, Mr. Wilson & Mr. Watkin's General Store. There was plenty of new money and lots of places to spend it.

Like groundhogs in March, new plantation houses popped up all over the rolling foothills of Caswell County. Each one needed cabinetry work and furniture. Woodworkers were in top demand, especially since there were no cities nearby where planters could buy fancy sofas, chests, chairs, and beds.

We don't know the details of Tom's first job in Milton, but as an African American, life may have been tense for him at first. White people in all of the slave states were suspicious of the growing free black population. They were afraid that free blacks might help the slaves rebel. They also resented business competition from trained artisans like Tom.

White folks in Caswell County might have

been even more hostile because Tom was literate. In 1810 more than half the adults of Caswell couldn't read, write, add, or subtract. Tom's education must have been as irritating as a splinter to them.

But the townspeople soon noticed his fine character. He became known as "a first rate workman, a remarkably sober, steady and industrious man. . . ." And he probably benefited from times when white and black society mingled, especially at religious gatherings.

After America's second great religious awakening in the early 1800s, traveling preachers held revivals throughout the South. These camp meetings, as they were called, caused a stir of religion in Caswell County. Often advertised in the Milton newspaper, they were open to all. Enslaved and free, black and white—everyone spent the day together in worship. Like salt and pepper, each culture's sermons, hymns, prayers, and food complemented the other.

We know that Tom probably attended revivals during his early days in Milton, since he later remarked on one to his daughter. "The Greatest revival I Ever Knew in the south, 95 or 97 persons in Milton profesed conversion," he noted. "A Baptist Preacher—he hase been Preaching Every night & day for one month . . . I truly hope they may be faithful to the End." Throughout his years in Milton, the white community noticed Tom's devotion to the church and respected him as a "high minded, good and valuable citizen."

Doubtless, Tom had white friends and was close to some of the several hundred free blacks living in Caswell County. But if he ever felt relaxed about his free status, the icy hand of North Carolina law woke him up. Tom Day was a free black, but he was not a free person.

Every month he watched the local militia, the Milton Blues, drill on New Bridge Street. Tom wasn't allowed to join—North Carolina law stated that free Negroes could not serve in the military except as musicians. He couldn't bear witness against a white person in court. Worst of all, he couldn't collect money owed to him by whites unless he owned property. What could a free black do if he worked for someone who refused to pay his wages? How could Tom save for his own shop if people owed him money, but no one had to pay?

Worry scratched him like sandpaper. As he got closer to the dream of striking out on his own, North Carolina lawmakers tightened the screws that held free blacks in place. In 1826 they ruled that *no* free blacks could enter the state. Free blacks were "unfortunate and troublesome," the legislators fumed, "a public nuisance."

Those free blacks who crossed the state line and stayed more than twenty days paid a fine of $500. Ignoring the law meant arrest and enslavement for ten years. How could he marry Acquilla, Tom fretted, if she couldn't live with him in North Carolina?

By 1827 he was close to being an independent cabinetmaker and starting his life with Acquilla. But no place, it seemed, was safe for a free black. He could be kidnapped, robbed of his free papers, and sold into slavery in just a few hours.

Tom Day possessed plenty of common sense. Lots of folks in Caswell County, he reasoned, knew and liked him. Better to live where he already had friends than to take a chance as a stranger somewhere else. First he would start his own business in Milton. Then he would figure out a way to get married.

The Workshop Years
• 1827–1830 •

Every time Tom walked by the little frame building on Main Street, he felt a buyer's itch. The space was only eighteen feet by sixteen feet, but he could build a workbench along one wall, store a wheel lathe at one end, and hang tools from the ceiling beams. The shop would be as tight as a new shoe, but it would be his. Best of all, he would own property. If anyone owed him money, the law would allow him to collect.

In 1827 Tom plunked down five hundred and fifty dollars for his first workshop. If business went well he would build an addition. First, though, he had to construct the most important tool of all: a workbench. Tom's bench was only about twenty-eight inches from the ground. This meant he could look down on the piece as he was building it. He wouldn't have to hold his hand tools or his neck high up in the air.

Next he scouted around for a boy to help him on the lathe. He needed a young fellow with strong arms to turn the iron crank on

This great wheel lathe is similar to one that Tom Day might have used. *Winterthur Museum, Winterthur, Delaware.*

Tom might have used a wheel lathe or a foot-operated treadle lathe to turn the spiral legs of these nested tables. *North Carolina State Archives, Raleigh, North Carolina.*

the great wheel. The wheel then turned a pulley. The pulley turned the lathe, which held a chair leg in place and rotated it at high speed. Tom told the boy when to speed the wheel up and when to slow it down.

While the lathe rotated, Tom applied a razor-sharp tool like a knife or file to turn, or carve, the leg into fancy shapes. After he turned a chair leg it might look like spools, spirals, or even links of sausage. The operation went well until the boy's arm began to ache, the crank slowly rolled to a halt, and Tom had to urge his helper on.

As wood chips flew past Tom's ear and shavings foamed at his feet, his eye for design and his years of practice served him well. He wasn't just a carpenter or a **joiner**. When he stood in front of the lathe he was an artist.

Sometimes he turned a new design that pleased his expert eye. Then he would tell the boy to stop the lathe so he could make a pattern, or template, out of wood. Tom hung the template on the wall and used it to make the same design whenever he needed it.

Tom knew he wasn't the only cabinet-maker in town, so he polished his business skills. He set low prices, made a supply of furniture to show (Beds were his specialty—

Tom mixed four kinds of wood and two furniture styles to make this bed. It has Empire-style legs and a Cottage-style headboard and footboard. *North Carolina State Archives, Raleigh, North Carolina.*

Tom Day advertises his shop in 1827. *North Carolina State Archives, Raleigh, North Carolina.*

he once made an extra-wide one for a three-hundred-pound woman), and did repair work. Always polite, "Thomas Day, Cabinetmaker" thanked his customers for their business in the *Milton Gazette* newspaper in March 1827. "All orders," he promised, "will be thankfully received and punctually attended to."

When a baby was born, the parents bought a cradle from Thomas Day. When someone died, the family came to him for a coffin. He even made custom fishing poles.

Soon planters asked him to complete whole rooms of furniture. This required traveling to the house, where he carefully measured the height of the ceiling and width and length of each room. Then he made pasteboard miniatures of the furniture to show the master and mistress. In the early years of his business most people wanted a plain style of furniture. Tom's simple country designs fit their tastes.

Thomas Day, the cabinetmaker, was busy and satisfied. He was doing what he liked to do and doing it well. Success, however, brought loneliness. He stood with one foot in the black world and one foot in the white world, but he couldn't rest himself in either one.

Lack of schooling and strict laws kept most free blacks in the South living in poverty. Tom felt blessed that he was spared the suffering of other free persons. He knew he would never end up in the Caswell County poorhouse. But when he thought about the dungeon and grate underneath the Caswell courthouse jail, he remembered that he, too, lived on a high wire. How easily he could fall off and tumble into slavery!

Tom was equal to or better than most whites in skill, education, and earning power. He had fit into their world and become part of their economic system. His income and the light skin he had inherited gave him much in common with white society. The citizens of Milton were friends, fellow churchgoers, and loyal customers. But he was still in their power. The laws always gave them the last word.

Years later he told his daughter what he thought of Milton's social world. "You have read in the scriptures how the two first Brothers Cain & Abel Enjoid Each others Society and how also the Patriarch David loved his beautiful son Absalom & you see the modern-time network [of] society, also— how frail the affection of Friends—how deceitful . . ." In the Bible stories of Cain and Absalom, both men murdered their brothers. Their betrayal may have reminded Tom of his own troubles with false-hearted friends.

He was pulled in two directions. Helpful to everybody, he may have trusted no one. Tom followed the same advice that he would later give to his daughter: "Well, you must love the lord thy God with thy whole heart, soul and strength and thy neighbor as thyself," he told her, "but all the time Worship God only." He read the Bible, kept his thoughts to himself, and turned his eyes toward Halifax County and the lovely Acquilla.

Tom and Acquilla Day became members of the Milton Presbyterian Church in 1841. He made these poplar pews for the church and may have been one of its ruling elders. *Jim Bridges.*

The Master Years
• 1830–1848 •

Eighteen-thirty was a remarkable year for Tom Day. Once he made up his mind, nothing could stop him from being with the woman he loved. With his heart racing like water in the mill creek, he returned to Halifax County at the beginning of the year. On Wednesday, January 6, Thomas Day married Acquilla Wilson.

The couple knew that North Carolina law forbade her from moving across the state line to live with her husband, so Tom decided to move himself and his business back to Halifax County, Virginia. Virginia laws were more strict than those of North Carolina—at least in North Carolina he could still vote. But what good was his growing pile of money if he couldn't be with Acquilla?

Tom was well respected in Milton. His successful shop brought status to the town. Alarmed that they might lose him, white residents quickly sent a petition to "the Honorable General Assembly of the State of North Carolina" in Raleigh. "Acquilla Wilson . . . [was] a woman of color of good family and character," the Miltonites declared. They asked the lawmakers to pass a bill. It would give "said Acquilla the privilege of migrating to the State free from fines and penalties. . . ."

When the honorable gentlemen of the assembly heard the petition, there must have been much coughing throughout the chamber. The men stewed. The 1826 law had been passed to control free negroes. Now they were supposed to pass another law that would break the first law!

Then they noticed that the attorney general for the state of North Carolina had attached a letter to the petition. Romulus Saunders was from Caswell County, and he wrote that Tom was a "Free man of color of very fair character, an excellent mechanic, industrious, honest and sober in his habits. . . ." The lawmakers hooked their thumbs behind their wide lapels, harrumphed a few more times, and passed the bill.

Tom and his bride were relieved. Acquilla moved to Milton, and they began their family. Their first child, Mary Ann, was born in 1831. Two sons, Devereaux and Thomas, Jr., followed in 1833 and 1837. At some point

Tom's mother, Morning Star, moved from Virginia to Caswell County. Some say she lived on a two-hundred-acre farm outside of town, where she would have grown wheat, corn, and, of course, tobacco.

The 1830 census shows that Thomas Day was truly an unusual man. Not only was he a free person living in a slave state, he was wealthy when most free people of color were grits-for-supper poor. He was a black artisan who trained white apprentices. And he owned two slaves.

Tom was not the only free black to become a slaveholder. There were four others in Caswell County in 1830, and one hundred and ninety-eight throughout the state. Most held under ten slaves, but two free blacks owned as many as forty-four slaves.

Sometimes prosperous free blacks bought slaves to protect them from mistreatment by others. Or slaves were purchased, then allowed to earn money and buy their own freedom. Many slaves owned by free blacks were members of the family. They were bought, then later set free.

But like white slaveholders, Tom's motive was profit. White artisans often refused to teach slaves, so they were apprenticed to another slave or a free black like Tom to learn a trade. After training a young man to make furniture, Tom would have been reluctant to see him leave when the apprenticeship was over. If he then bought the slave, he had free labor. He also had a trained, but captive, workforce for his shop.

It is true that free blacks who owned slaves helped keep the cruel practice alive. But Tom may have felt the laws for free blacks were so strict that he must make money by any necessary means. Perhaps he would have bought and trained a white apprentice if he could have done so. Since only black slavery existed in America, he made what he thought was a practical choice.

Like pecans in a pie, people always want to rise to the top. Slavery made that simple. The first Africans had been delivered to Virginia in 1619. Since then, American society had layered itself with slaves on the bottom, then free blacks, poor landless whites and small farmers next, and finally wealthy planters covering all.

This caste system encouraged free blacks like Tom to keep themselves apart from slaves. "Charge them to be careful . . . with slaves & not to deal with them," wrote a county justice about a free black family in Virginia in 1823, "otherwise they would & ought to forfeit the good opinion which the people are disposed to entertain of them." Tom was caught in the middle layer of society. That helped him forget that he had enslaved those underneath.

In 1839 farmers in the North Carolina piedmont grew seventeen million pounds of tobacco. As the white slaveholders of Milton and Caswell County prospered, so did Tom's business. The desire for grand homes continued.

The Greek Revival style that had been so popular in Europe finally arrived in the South. Tall white columns on the outside of plantation houses reminded the owners of ancient Greek temples. Matching woodwork and furniture on the inside made them feel like kings and queens.

In 1838 Tom built the mantels, stairs, newel post, and cabinets for a house called Woodside. Still standing, Woodside is a Greek Revival manor two miles outside of Milton. It is typical of the homes built in Caswell County during the boom years.

At Woodside a master carpenter erected massive Doric columns to hold up the roof

The Doric columns on the porch at Woodside are the simplest style of Greek columns. *Paul Collinge.*

Tom Day made this table supported by pillars, its scrolled feet shaped like the top of an Ionic column. *North Carolina State Archives, Raleigh, North Carolina.*

of the front porch. Tom continued the same theme inside. To make the ten mantels throughout the house, he followed Greek Revival designs, probably from a pattern book called *The Architect, or Practical House Carpenter*.

Two plain square Doric columns support the mantel in the "everyday" parlor. This room was used to receive ordinary visitors. Curved Ionic columns hold up the mantel in the more feminine "ladies" parlor, which was saved for special occasions.

Furniture fashions changed to suit the Greek Revival architectural style. Books of furniture patterns like *The Cabinetmaker's Assistant* helped Tom keep up with the new shapes. Pillar and scroll furniture imitated the curves of an Ionic column. No doubt the owners of Woodside asked him to make some pieces in this popular style, and he obliged.

His co-workers may have done the plain work for the house, such as hanging closets and built-in cupboards. But it was Thomas Day who made the magnificent newel post at Woodside. Like an aged warrior, the coiled mahogany post watches over the house and all who enter.

Tom probably followed a pattern book to construct the Woodside newel post. This post and others like it throughout Caswell County are variations of the "thumb," or curved Ionic style. But one humanlike newel post in a Caswell County home surprises the eye. It resembles a wooden statue made in West Africa.

Both the African artist and Tom Day cut sharp angles into the wood to suggest a person's body. Neither tried to copy the real shape of a body, but only hinted at certain parts: head, neck, breasts, belly, knees, feet, and spine. African sculptors often exaggerate some body parts to show their importance.

The newel post at Woodside plantation. The round design on the side of the stairs matches the curve of the post. *Jim Bridges.*

This snakelike newel post is in the Bartlett Yancy house in Milton, North Carolina. *Jim Bridges.*

The head is made large to represent the mind. Oversized feet and bent knees show calm strength and cool steadiness. The African statue displays all these features, and Tom's post appears to do the same.

There are other similarities. Both Tom and the African artist carefully chose one large piece of wood to carve. To avoid ruining the piece, each stopped to measure his progress. Like Tom with his vertical handsaw, the African used a hand tool such as an adze and tried to avoid a slip of the hand.

The African artist might have polished his statue with leaves, dipped it in a mud bath, or treated it with sap. Tom also proudly oiled and polished his creations. No doubt both men were pleased with their work. "I am as happy doing it," Tom once said about woodworking, "as I shall ever be anywhere."

Sometime during the 1850s, Tom sculpted a pair of faces for a mantel. These, too, resemble art made in West Africa. The following description of an African mask [from *Bambara Sculpture of the Western Sudan*] could easily fit Tom's twin faces:

The eyes of the mask are large, so that [the god] may see and uncover everything; the nos-

The newel post from a staircase of the Paschal house in Milton. *North Carolina State Archives, Raleigh, North Carolina.*

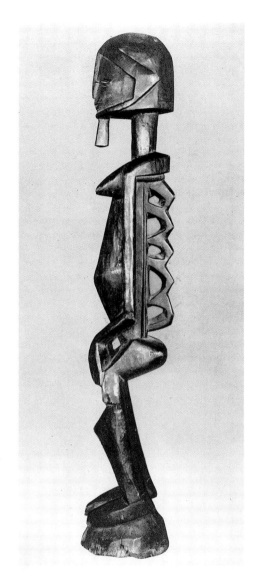

Thirty inches high, this statue represents the spirit of the artist's family. The bent knees and straight arms give the figure a cool, calm appearance. *Walker Evans Estate.*

The faces Tom Day sculpted frightened the owner's daughter, who, according to a family member, refused to practice the piano while alone in the room. The cap and collar give this face an odd clownlike look. Photograph on left: *Paul Collinge*. Photograph on right: *Jim Bridges*.

trils are wide open, for he must sense every-thing and smell the good and evil of all things. The mouth is twisted, since [the god] does not talk but only whistles and sings. The chin of the mask is square, as a sign of purity, decision and clairvoyance.

African masks often bear the features of an ancestor. They are used in religious cere-monies to invoke the spirit of the deceased. Like the African artist, Tom may have had a particular person in mind when he carved the stern faces. Or perhaps their fearsome look expressed an emotion hidden deep within Tom's soul.

We will never know Thomas Day's thoughts as he chiseled the startling features of the faces. And we can never be sure that any of his unusual carvings are directly re-lated to Africa. International slave trade had legally ended in America in 1807 when Tom was six years old. But captured Africans con-tinued to arrive on illegal slave ships throughout his lifetime. It is not impossible that Tom Day would have seen woodwork made by an African artist or a descendant of an African. If so, Tom held on to the mem-ory, then turned it into an African-American vision of his own.

Jim Bridges.

The Tavern Years
• 1848–1857 •

It seemed to Tom that he was always apologizing for being late. On January 5, 1848, he wrote to the president of the debating society at the University of North Carolina at Chapel Hill: "I am sorry truly that there has been so much Disappointment about the Blinds. you will perceive they were shipped the 8th August. [Dan] river has been very low from the great Drought and little arriving."

He wrote to another customer, "I would have sent the chair to Danville before this time but for the press of Orders. . . . I have been completely crowded with orders."

When Tom stood in his little shop, he knew why he was always behind in his work. Years earlier he had built a twelve foot by twelve foot addition. But the space was still a cramped confusion of tools and benches, six chimneys, eight cabinetmakers (three black and five white), and one white laborer. Something had to be done.

Tom was as happy as a peeper frog in a pond when he bought the Yellow Tavern on Main Street in 1848. Built in 1815, the brick building was one of the finest in the county. Sunbursts of glass and metal crowned the three front doors. Two great rooms opened off the center hall on the bottom floor, and there were two large bedchambers upstairs. Twenty-four feet by fifty-four feet, it was big enough to hold his family and a showroom.

Tom constructed a two-story wing out of wood on the right side of the tavern. Twenty feet by seventy-five feet, this was his new workshop and office. There would be room to add a steam-powered wood-drying kiln outside the shop and room for all his workers on the inside. Now Thomas Day, the cabinetmaker, could finally fill his orders on time.

By the time Tom finished remodeling, the entire structure had two stoves, five chimneys, and twelve fireplaces. He was relieved to find better housing for his family. His daughter, Mary Ann, had hated the old shop. She explained her younger brother's reckless behavior to her mother: "It is not to be wondered at that D[evereaux] is so depraved when you consider he has been raised in a shop of the meanest of God's creations. . . ."

Her father was insulted. He argued back,

"You greatly mistake the character of this shop and the hands. there is not a more respectable house of the kind in my knowledge and no hands as laborers have a higher credit than ours."

The craftsman defended his shop and his workers. As a parent, though, he knew that Mary Ann needed a better class of young people than Milton could offer. He didn't approve of their poor schooling and uppity ways.

"Beautiful young Ladies are lost to all usefulness by a lack of proper information," he said. "There is now a perfect Waste of human flesh here in the verry way the young Ladies come into Village to School—they learn a little of one thing a little of another and a little on Piano—they return to their country homes knowing nothing but a scoff at persons who they think inferior to themselves & with nothing in their heads but foolish pride."

Tom had lost all patience with Milton's snobs. Perhaps some of the foolish young ladies had scoffed at his dear Mary Ann. He decided that she deserved a better life. "I want you to be in some place whare your turn of feelings & manner can be well met," he said. "& I fully Expect to affect my purpose if I live long enough."

Even the adults made Tom weary. He must have felt affection for his friends and some of his customers, but he was secretly disgusted with the shallow nature of others. "They cant—Write—they wont read—," he complained. "They are something they cant tell what—They Keep Clear of Poor people & follow after rich people—"

Tom was a diplomat. He knew he could share these feelings only with his family, not with the white folks of Milton. To them Tom was a "respectable negro" who would inform them of rumors of slave uprisings. "In the event of any disturbance among the blacks," one Miltonite said, Tom would act as a go-between.

Sometimes it seemed that each member of his family was like an animal on a very long leash. They could pretend to live as if they had no limits. But they were free blacks, and the leash would yank them back if they went too far.

In 1835 Tom's right to vote had been taken away. (As a woman, Acquilla had never been allowed to vote.) By 1840 he could not keep a gun without a license. In 1844 free black

The Yellow Tavern built in 1815. *Jim Bridges*.

children could no longer legally attend school.

Perhaps this law helped Tom decide to send Mary Ann to school in the North. By 1847, his sixteen-year-old daughter had already received some education at a private academy in Wilbraham, Massachusetts. Though the law forbade it, there was one free black attending school in Caswell County in 1850. If this was one of Tom's sons, racial harassment may have forced him to complete his education in the North. By 1851 all of Tom's children were enrolled in the same school in Massachusetts.

Both Tom and Acquilla deeply missed their children, especially Mary Ann. "Your mother is still quite well, but complaining a little," Tom wrote. "She wants to se[e] you very badly & so do I—"

Letters from Tom to Mary Ann at school tell of his private feelings about Milton, his profession, and his children. Like any father Tom worried about their school performance. His firstborn son was a disappointment. Tom heard that Devereaux had been careless with money. Exasperated, he commented to Mary Ann that "Devereaux, I am sorry to know, was the worst boy I ever had

to manage in my life." There is no mention of Thomas Day, Jr., in the letters, so Tom's namesake must have stayed out of trouble.

Tom clearly saved his highest hopes for his oldest child. "Learn to walk well—to stand Erect," he told Mary Ann. "Learn to feel free & to feel well & easy." The proud father wanted her to have every advantage, even a trip to Europe. "I intend to get you a Piano and am in hopes you will learn to play on the Guitar so to amuse yourself while traveling perhaps on the Broad Ocean."

He admitted that life in Milton left much to be desired. "Thare is nothing here but to make a little money & that but little to induce us to stay here—," he said to Mary Ann. Then he tried to cheer her up about coming home. "Tho with all this you will Enjoy yourself well as any whare for awhile—"

The air that free blacks breathed became more poisonous with every passing decade. In the 1850s, mob violence against free negroes grew worse in North Carolina. Tom must have been anxious. He thought about leaving Milton altogether. "My great concirn at this time & will be," he wrote, "is to get some sootable place for you and your Brothers—us all—to settle down. . . ." But how

Tom often glued thin, wide strips of expensive mahogany, called veneer, to a carcass of cheaper wood. *Jim Bridges*.

could he leave his shop and his business? And what about Morning Star? She was eighty-five and too old for a move.

He had mixed feelings about leaving. "I can tell you it will not be [a] verry great while before I hope to leave Milton," he wrote. Two paragraphs later he said, "I am perfectly satisfied as regards Milton." Because of the laws, Tom could not call himself a citizen of the town. Still, it had been home for over half of his life.

The Final Years
• 1858–1861 •

When the 1850s began, Tom could not have guessed that they would end in ruin. These were peak production years at his shop. A steam-powered circular saw quickly turned logs into planks of wood. The steam-powered kiln speeded up the drying process—no longer did he have to wait one year per inch for planks to dry. Tom's estate was worth $8,000 in 1850, including seventy thousand board feet of wood. With twelve workers, he was now one of the largest furniture producers in the state.

The tobacco bonanza continued in the North Carolina piedmont. Production of the bright yellow, slow-cured weed almost tripled during the 1850s. By the end of the decade there were eleven tobacco factories in Caswell County alone.

New businesses sprouted like corn all over Milton. Folks bought ready-made shoes to wear to dance lessons, ordered fancy hats to wear to horse races, and purchased sweets from the candy store to eat in the lobby of the Milton Hotel.

Tom knew his own business was too profitable to leave. He resigned himself to staying in Milton and felt at peace about it. "My highest pleasure is in discharge of my Every day duty as nearly as possible," he said. Throughout the decade his orders increased, including a large number from a former governor of the state, David Reid. In 1857 one of Tom's tables received an award at North Carolina's Fifth Annual Fair.

But by 1858 his business was as shaky as an old chair. He desperately needed cash to pay his bills. Tom had established credit with businesses in New York and Baltimore that sold imported mahogany. But he couldn't pay them until his customers paid him.

A packing crate addressed to Tom Day was used for the sides of this Empire chest. *Courtesy of Mr. and Mrs. Bill Richardson. Photograph North Carolina Museum of History, Raleigh, North Carolina.*

An 1858 advertisement in the *Milton Gazette and Roanoke Advertiser. North Carolina State Archives, Raleigh, North Carolina.*

In rural places like Milton, people often traded goods instead of paying for them. In exchange for furniture Tom may have accepted a horse, for example. And when people did pay him with cash, they often waited up to ten years to finally settle the bill.

In 1857 there had been a financial panic in America. Everyone wanted their money at the same time. Tom was pinched in two places at once—by creditors in the North and debtors in the South.

People in Milton were casual about debts. In 1858 the executor of an estate placed an advertisement in the *Milton Chronicle*. "Persons indebted to said estate will come forward like Gentlemen," the ad stated. "Come up boys, settle and make things easy." Debts were a matter of a gentleman's honor. But did that honor apply when the gentleman was indebted to a free black?

Even in Caswell County, the well-liked Thomas Day might have been a victim of fear. In sixteen North Carolina counties, including Caswell, more than half the population was now African American. Whites were in the minority. Some were almost hysterical with hate. They thought that all free blacks should be forced to leave the state.

Those who owed Tom money might have felt too hostile to pay. As a free black, there was little he could do to force them.

One early spring morning in 1858, Tom walked down to the newspaper office. He placed an advertisement to sell his ready-made stock of furniture. "Money is greatly desired by the proprietor," he stated, "and for cash good bargains may be expected."

But even the offer to deliver coffins "at very short notice" could not help Tom's business. In 1859 his shop, tools, land, horses, and slaves named Jim, Peter, Davy, Mark, and Julia, were to be sold at public auction. Then Tom's reliable son, Thomas, Jr., signed a promise that he would run the business and pay his father's debts. Tom Day's property was now reduced to $4,000, but Tom, Jr., managed to operate the shop until 1871.

In 1859 the noose tightened around the free black's neck. The North Carolina Supreme Court said a free negro could strike a white man in self-defense, but only if the white man tried to kill him first. No one in Milton would harm him, Tom was sure. But he couldn't predict what might happen when he traveled outside of his home county.

This photograph was given to the *Baltimore Afro-American* newspaper as a picture of Tom Day. The youthful face and 1860s style of dress indicate that it is probably a picture of Tom Day's youngest son, Tom Day, Jr. *Courtesy Mary Satterfield.*

Tom must have felt discouraged by the growing racial tension. And he was weakened by the embarrassment of possible bankruptcy. He had suffered from what he called "afflictions" for several years. "We have been very much disappointed in getting work put up," he had written to a customer in another town in 1858, "my own health preventing very much."

As with the early years of Tom's life, there is no record of his final days. It is believed

An African-American garden club in Caswell County, North Carolina, erected this marker in 1977. Within the rock enclosure two small unmarked stones lie at the head and foot of what local legend says is Tom Day's grave. *Mary E. Lyons*.

that the talented artisan died at the age of sixty in 1861. There were 761 deaths from consumption, or tuberculosis, in North Carolina in 1860. Perhaps Tom passed away from this contagious and lingering disease. Local tradition says he is buried on a farm two miles from Milton.

Thomas Day was well known throughout North Carolina and Virginia. But the outbreak of the Civil War in April of 1861 may have obscured news of his death. We have no announcement or obituary to record the reaction of his fellow North Carolinians.

Many pieces of his furniture survive, however. They are an elegant testimony to his craftsmanship. Tom didn't sign his work, but it is easy to identify his furniture. Like a creative cook who alters a recipe, he added his own unique flavor to popular styles.

To please customers Tom, the craftsman, kept up with changing fashions in furniture. To suit his own tastes Tom, the artist, carved distinctive newel posts and mantels. Both the graceful furniture and unusual woodwork are his special gifts to us. They prove that even the choking laws of oppression could not diminish the power of this African-American artist.

Tom Day may have made this post in the shape of his initials. *Mary E. Lyons.*

The Yellow Tavern following the 1989 fire. It is now a National Historic Landmark and is being restored as a museum and community gathering place. *Jim Bridges.*

AFTERWORD

On a windy day in 1989, sparks from a pile of burning trash blew onto the Yellow Tavern. The wooden structure and its sawdust insulation quickly ignited. Seven volunteer fire departments used the town's entire water supply to try to save the building. But all that remained of it was a broken shell of brick and plaster, some blackened timbers, and the ashes of 174 years of history.

The bustling pre–Civil War town of Milton is now a sleepy little village of 191 people. A lonely traffic light (the only one in the county) swings at the crest of Main Street. Thomas Day's furniture, however, is still proudly displayed in local homes. When a piece of Day furniture is sold to someone outside the county, residents mourn as if a dear old friend has moved away.

The state of North Carolina is also proud of Tom Day. The furniture that he made for the governor is on permanent display in Raleigh at the North Carolina Museum of History. The public television film *Civil War: The North Carolina Story* includes a segment on Tom Day. When the Museum of Early Southern Decorative Arts in Winston-Salem held an exhibit of Tom's furniture in 1991, he was called a "rare individual" with "superb skills."

Over one hundred years after Tom's death, his spirit is still alive. Most histories of antebellum African Americans note the life and works of Thomas Day. He continues to teach us about the lives of free blacks during the years of slavery, the craft of making furniture, and the beauty of African-American art.

GLOSSARY

Bench dog   A small round plug of wood inserted into the workbench. The bench dog keeps a plank of wood from sliding off the bench when sanding or planing.

Donkey's ear   A board with an angled edge of 45 degrees used to cut another board at the same angle.

Dovetail   Interlocking joint that connects two pieces of wood at right angles. Pins shaped like the tail of a dove are cut out of the end of one board. Then, like pieces of a puzzle, they are fitted into dovetail-shaped cuts on the end of the other board.

Joiner   A carpenter who can make the variety of joints necessary to build furniture.

Mortise and tenon   The joint created when a rectangular plug on one board fills a rectangular hole in another board.

Rabbet   A "lip" cut along the edge of a board. Two boards can be joined when their rabbeted edges, or "lips," are fitted, then glued together.

Slat   Narrow horizontal pieces of wood that are joined to the posts of a chair. Slats look like the rungs of a ladder. Hence the name, ladder-back chair.

Splat   A vertical piece of wood that joins the top of the chair to the seat. A splat can be carved to look like a vase, a shield, or even a harp.

SELECTED SOURCES

A few of the books and articles used to research the life of Tom Day:

Barfield, Rodney. "Thomas Day, Cabinetmaker." *Nineteenth Century* (Autumn 1976): 23–32.

Franklin, John Hope. *The Free Negro in North Carolina 1790–1860.* Chapel Hill: The University of North Carolina Press, 1943.

Goldwater, Robert. *Bambara Sculpture from*

the Western Sudan. New York: The Museum of Primitive Art, 1960.

Johnson, Guion Griffis. *Ante-Bellum North Carolina: A Social History.* Chapel Hill: The University of North Carolina Press, 1937.

Leuzinger, Elsy. *The Art of Black Africa.* Barcelona, Spain: Ediciónes Poligrafa, 1985.

Nicholls, Michael L. "Passing Through This Troublesome World: Free Blacks in the Early Southside." *The Virginia Magazine of History and Biography* 92 (January 1984): 50–70.

Powell, William S. *When the Past Refused to Die: A History of Caswell County, 1777–1977.* Durham, North Carolina: Moore Publishing Company, 1977.

Robinson, W. A. and others. "Thomas Day and His Family." *The Negro History Bulletin* 8 (March 1950): 123–126, 140.

Watson, Aldren A. *Country Furniture.* New York: Thomas Y. Crowell Company, 1974.

Tom Day made the newel post, but the gold finial was a later addition. *Jim Bridges.*

INDEX

Page numbers for illustrations are in *italics*

African art, 23–27
apprenticeships, 4, 5, 8, 19–20
artistry, Tom's, 7, 14–15, 37

background, Tom's, 3–5
beds, *15*, 15–16
business, 15–16, 28, 32, 33–34

chairs, *6*, 14–15
character, Tom's, 11, 17
childhood, Tom's, 1, 5
children, Tom's, 19, 28–31
columns, *2–3*, 20–23, *21, 22*

Day, Acquilla Wilson, 9, 12, 18–19, 31
Day, Devereaux (Tom's son), 19, 28, 31
Day, Mary Ann (Tom's daughter), 19, 28, 29, 31
Day, Morning Star (Tom's mother), 3–5, 19, 32
Day, Thomas, Jr. (Tom's son), 19, 31, 35, *35*
Day, Tom. *See* specific topics
Day, Tom (Tom's father), 4–5
death, Tom's, 35–37, *36*

education, 10–11, 17, 29–31
Tom's, 3, 4

faces, Tom's carvings, 24–27, *26, 27*
free blacks, 3–4, 19–20, 39
restrictions on, 7–9, 11–12, 17, 29–32
and whites, 10–11, 34–35
furniture, 5–6, 10, 22–23, 39
decoration of, *6, 9, 22*

Greek Revival style, 20–23, *21*

indentured servants, 4, 6–7

journeyman, Tom as, 7, 10–12

lathes, 12–15, *13*
laws, 4
and free blacks, 6–9, 11–12, 17, 18–19, 29–32

mantels, *2*, 22, 24
marriage, 9, 12, 18
Milton, town of, 9, 10, 17, 39
Tom and, 18–19, 29–32, 33
miniatures, 8, 19

newel posts, *23*, 23–25, *24, 25, 37, 41*
North Carolina, 10, 33, 39
and free blacks, 18–19, 31, 34, 35

religion, 11, 17, 18

slavery, 4–5, 7, 17, 19–20, 27
styles, 23–27
of furniture, *15*, 17, 20, 22–23, 37

tobacco production, 10, 20, 33
tools, *vi, 1*, 24, 32

Virginia, 7, 18–19
voting, 18, 29

wealth, 10, 33
Tom's, 17, 19–20, 31, 32, 33–34, 34–35
whites, 17, 29
and free blacks, 10–11, 34–35
Woodside (mansion), 20–23, *21*
woodworking, 1, 5, *32*, 32
Tom's feelings about, 17, 24
Tom's training in, 4, 5, 7, 9
workshops, Tom's, 12, 28–29, *30, 38*

Yellow Tavern, the, 28–29, *30, 38*, 39